Tails of
Gus & Fanny
The Farmhouse

Dedication

To our cats

Acknowledgments

The characters in this book are fictional, but there are some facts involved, too. Various historical events surrounding the farmhouse were used in this story.

We thank our families for their love and support throughout this project.

Written by Patti Truedson Higgins

Illustrated by Teresa Weismann Knight

Edited by John Knight

ISBN-13: 978-1492872177

ISBN-10: 1492872172

Prologue

Patti Truedson Higgins, author, and Teresa Weismann Knight, illustrator of this book, both planned to leave on vacation at the same time. Previously, they had watched each other's cats while one of them was away.

Forced to find a solution to the dilemma, they decided to set up their cats with all of the necessities needed for a short stay in Patti's farmhouse.

One problem existed. Patti and Teresa were friends, but the cats were not. They decided to separate the two cats, sequestering one upstairs, the other downstairs.

As they walked away, the friends turned to look back at the house, wondering aloud what their cats were talking about and what was going to happen while they were gone . . . thus the "Tails of Gus & Fanny" was born.

Purr Purr

Gus let his guard down and sprawled like a limp dishrag across Peggy's lap. The big tomcat was on break.

"It's so sad. This old place is falling down around us, Gus," said Peggy. She pulled at a weed seed stuck in his fur. Gus lifted his head and looked at her. "Sorry," Peggy went back to petting him. "I can't wait until we have the money to turn this house back into the jewel of the county. It is a historical monument after all." She kissed the top of his head and whispered into his ear, "Then Rob and I can get out of our teeny-tiny apartment and move in here with you." A horn honked outside, "There's Rob. I have to go now, Gus." Peggy looked at her watch. "Tess is late. I'm going to miss her. Oh well, can't be helped. I'm counting on you to take care of the place for me. I love you, Gus." She slid the cat from her lap onto the warm space she left on the worn, brown chaise lounge, then disappeared down the stairs of the farmhouse.

"I certainly will," meowed Gus. He reached his head around to lick a spot on his back. "Yes siree, Bob, Gus is on the job." He stretched out on his side and watched tree branches swaying in the wind outside the window. "I love you too, Peggy." He heard the familiar bang of the backdoor, the thud of a car door, the whir of a motor, then the crunching of gravel as tires rolled down the driveway. *See you later, Peggy,* he thought. *I'll just take a short catnap. What can it hurt?* His eyes drooped and closed.

Gus was sneaking through the tall grass after a tiny vole. He was within two inches of the little critter. He carefully crouched on his hind quarters, sprung forward paws and claws out, and a door slammed. Gus woke with a start and shook the sleep from his head. He listened to banging and shuffling noises coming from downstairs. "What's that?" he asked and trotted to the bottom of the staircase. He pushed against the door, but the door would not open. "Odd. Why is this door latched?" More unfamiliar movements came from the other side of the door. Gus sniffed the air and roared, "STRANGERS!" He stood on his hind legs and pushed with both paws, but the door would not open. He roared again, "PEGGY, STRANGERS!" He dashed to the top of the stairs where he spied an unfamiliar vehicle through the window. He hissed and spat at the window as he watched the human intruder get into the car and drive away. "And don't come back!"

A bloodcurdling yow shot up from downstairs. Gus's fur stood up, Mohawk-style, along his back.

Humph Humph

Earlier that day at her home with Tess and Jack, Fanny had followed her nose to the intoxicating aroma of canned tuna fish in her bowl. *I wonder if this is some kind of trick?* She scanned the garage then circled the bowl of oily fish several times watching for danger. Finally satisfied the coast was clear, she dipped her head deep in the bowl, closed her eyes, and took a bite. Faster than a speeding bullet, Tess scooped her up and stuffed her into her carrying cage, and BANG, the door was closed and latched.

Tess looked into the cage and smiled. "You're going on an adventure."

Fanny hissed and growled, "Adventure!"

Tess loaded the cage into her car. She looked in at Fanny and asked, "Comfy in your pet taxi?"

"Humph!" Fanny turned her tail to Tess and swished it. "Humph!" she said again.

Tess got in the car and drove down the road. When she finally stopped, carried the cage into the house and opened the door, Fanny bolted out. She skidded to a stop under a wooden cabinet and commenced to quiver and yowl with gusto.

"Be a good kitty," said Tess.

"Good kitty," said Fanny. "I AM A SUPERIOR FELINE!" she yowled.

Tess didn't try to coax Fanny out from under the cabinet. In fact, she bent over, looked at her cat, and said, "I'm sorry, Fanny, but this place will just have to do. I'm sure you'll be very comfortable here."

Fanny heard Tess walk out of the house and shut the door. She heard a motor start and Tess's car driving down the driveway. She stayed put under the cabinet, wound tight, ready to dart away if need be. She puffed up and gave a few more healthy yowls then listened. The house was quiet, save for the hum of a refrigerator motor and the leaves of a tree rustling in the breeze outside. She finally began to relax. She licked her dainty white paws and smoothed the fur on her face. Her stomach started rumbling. Crouching close to the floor, and extending one paw at a time, she crept out from under her hiding place. She followed worn trails in the carpet from room to room. *Not exactly the Ritz,* she thought looking around. Her face squinched up, her nose twitched, and she sneezed. *Someone certainly needs to vacuum up all this dust.* She found a large bowl of kitty kibble and another bowl full of water. *Dry cat food! Tess surely doesn't expect me to eat this?* She turned her nose up in the air and stepped away. Her stomach rumbled again. *Where is my tuna fish, anyway? I'm going to give her a piece of my mind when she comes back!*

Padding about through the rooms on the first floor of the old house searching for an exit, she spied a box of cat litter. *Thank heavens this place has a proper lavatory!* she thought. She found three closed doors. She sniffed under the first and smelled fresh air. She pushed against it, but it wouldn't budge. She trotted to the second, sniffed fresh air, pushed against it, but it wouldn't budge, either. She sniffed at the bottom of the third door. "CAT!" she yowled and darted as far back under the cabinet as she could go. *Oh gross, spider webs*! She shook her paws then swiped at the dusty webs that clung to her whiskers.

Yeow Yeow

Gus had, of course, been sitting at the bottom of the stairs listening to Fanny. When Fanny's pink nose sniffed under the door he bristled and yelled. "CAT! What are you doing in my house? GET OUT RIGHT NOW!"

Fanny readied herself for a knockdown, drag-out cat fight.

"SCAT!" said Gus.

Nothing happened. Fanny padded out of her hiding place, cocked her head to the side and stared at the door. "Come out here and make me!"

 Gus hissed.

Fanny snickered. She looked at her pet taxi sitting in the middle of the room. "Tess brought me here this morning and she'll be back any time now, so don't worry your big, dumb head over me. I don't want to stay in this dump any longer than I have to."

"DUMP? I'll have you know this farmhouse is a historical monument, well over one hundred years old. Now leave, vamoose, SCAT!"

Fanny took a couple steps closer to the door. "I think the dust under that cabinet is one hundred years old." She brought her paw to her mouth and licked it clean again.

Gus stood on his hind legs and leaned his front paws against the door. He puffed out his chest and tried to see the intruder through the keyhole of the door. "YOU don't BELONG here! You need to LEAVE right now!" His tail swished under the door. Fanny pounced at Gus's tail. Gus jumped down, yanked his tail back, and growled.

Fanny crouched on the floor and looked under the door. *Gray tiger stripe, how common,* she thought. She stuck her paw under the door and swatted at Gus's feet. "Like I said, I will gladly leave this decrepit place once my mistress comes back for me."

Gus saw her paw and slapped at it. He too crouched down and looked under the door. *Hmm, a calico princess, I should have known,* he thought. "Why are you HERE?"

"I could ask you the same question," said Fanny. "And, would you please stop yelling at me, it's annoying."

"I live here. But again I ask, why ARE you here and WHO are you?" said Gus.

Fanny stretched out on the floor and began to groom

her fur. "My name is Princess Fantas-ti-cat, but Tess and Jack call me Fanny. I don't know why I'm here." Fanny looked around the room. "I really don't know."

THUD! THUD! THUD! Heavy footsteps crossed the attic ceiling. Fanny bumped her head scurrying under the cabinet. "YOW!" she said rubbing her head with her paw.

Gus hung his head and stared up the stairs. "Great, just great. It's Fingers," he said.

"Who's Fingers?" said Fanny.

"GUS!" Fingers yelled.

"By the way, my name is Augustus," Gus said to Fanny, "but Peggy and Rob call me Gus".

More scratching and banging noises came from upstairs. "Well, Gus, this just keeps getting better and better," said Fanny.

Crack Crack

Gus looked at the golden light coming in the window at the top of the stairs. *It's the witching hour, time for goblins, ghouls, and pesky raccoons,* he thought and slowly climbed the stairs. Fingers' heavy footsteps on the ceiling had rained down a shower of dust into the room.

BANG, BANG, BANG! Fingers knocked at the attic door. "Hey, Gus! Why's this here door closed?"

Gus stopped at the top of the stairs. "Fingers! Hey! My main raccoon! Did you say the door is closed?" He heaved a sigh of relief.

Fingers banged on the door again. "It sure ain't open."

"I swear I didn't know it was. Peggy must have closed it."

"The boys are at da barn. There ain't no food there. The boss sent me down here ta see what's up. You ain't holding out on us, are you Gus?"

"Fingers, buddy, you know me better than that. You know I always share with you and the boys."

Fingers sniffed all around the closed door sending more dust flying through the cracks. "You got food in there?"

Gus looked around the room and spied a shiny new feeder full to the brim with red, yellow and brown kibble. "Sweet," said Gus.

"Sweet? What's sweet? Answer the question." Fingers held up his paws, wiggled his digits, and smiled admiring the gold ring on his pinky. Then he cracked his knuckles. "I can make short work of this here door."

TAILS OF GUS & FANNY

From the window above the chaise lounge, Gus saw three other masked bandits waddling toward the neighbor's yard. "Looks like your gang decided to raid the kitten's food on the deck next door."

Fingers smacked the attic door with a balled up fist. "I'll be back! Tony's gonna want ta collect his share of your food. I know you got food in there. Protection comes with a price, Gus. We put our lives on the line keepin' you and the rest of the neighborhood cats here safe." Fingers' fingers poked through the crack and wrapped around the door. He gave the door a good shake.

"I know you do, Fingers. I know." Gus said shaking his head right to left.

"Just so ya do." He pulled his paw back, twirled his pinky ring, and snarled, "Guess I'll mosey on over and join them. I'll be needing some sustenance. You know what that is?" He drummed his claws on the door.

Gus rolled his eyes. "Yes, I know what sustenance is. You need food."

"That's right. I need some good nourishment. Which, I might add, I'm not getting here tonight." He held the gold ring up to the light, blew on it, then rubbed it on his fur, held it up to the light again and smiled. "I'll be back, my friend."

Gus rolled his eyes again and thought, *my friend?*

Fingers waddled back across the attic where he climbed out through a moss-encrusted hole in the wall. He hopped down to the porch roof then slid down a drainpipe to a windowsill.

Fanny sat on the back of an old couch looking out the window listening to Gus and Fingers. She felt tired. It had been a long day. Her eyes were at half mast, somewhere between sleeping and awake. She had just settled her head on her paws when something caught her attention—movement at the corner of her eye. Fingers' face was less than an inch from hers on the outside of the glass window. She hissed and arched her back. Every hair on her body stood straight up as well as her tail.

Fingers fell from the windowsill laughing. He rolled on the ground holding his sides laughing. He shook his head and waddled off still laughing.

Fanny crouched on the back of the sofa snarling, "Scoundrel!"

The sun had set and a bright full moon was rising in the night sky. Fanny regained her composure, but kept a vigilant eye out the window. Upstairs Gus was looking out the window as well. He saw Fingers join the other raccoons on the neighbor's deck. He looked

up and noticed bats zigzag back and forth across the face of the moon.

"WHO? WHO?" Two big eyes blinked at Gus from a tree across the driveway. "WHO? WHO? It's YOU! YOU!"

"Smart aleck Owl!" said Gus.

The owl spread its wings, and as it flew past the window it screeched, "I SEE YOU, GUS!"

Gus ducked. "I see you too, Spike."

BUMP BUMP

This has been an awful, horrible, terrible day, thought Fanny. She silently padded into a large bedroom. *Ghastly house,* she sneezed. *Dust covers everything!* She hopped up on a big bed and nestled in on a soft crocheted afghan. *I can't believe Tess left me here! Surely Jack doesn't know about this!* She shook her head and tried to keep her eyes open. *I hope they come for me tomorrow.* She fell asleep.

The pale, shadowy apparitions of Hilma and her Siamese cat, Kit Kat, materialized in the bedroom with Fanny. Decades before, Hilma had been the mistress of the once glorious farmhouse. As the wife of the town's only doctor, Dr. R. X. Gitwell, she had hosted many lavish parties there. Her beauty and kindness made her the envy of the town. She and the good doctor were never blessed with children, so it was no wonder Hilma doted on her cat. Her reign as the town's social butterfly came to an abrupt end, however, when Dr. R. X. Gitwell mysteriously disappeared. Hilma closed the doors to the townspeople and lived the rest of her life shut up in her house with Kit Kat always by her side. When Kit Kat died she buried the cat in the basement and requested that, when her time came, she be buried beside her, so they could be together forever. As ghosts, she and Kit Kat haunted the house. They both loved Gus's company, but now there was an intruder.

Hilma hovered near the ceiling, her long gray hair gently waving about her head. She tapped her long fingernail on her front tooth, pivoting her head right and left, all the while staring at Fanny. Kit Kat began flying in circles batting at Fanny.

"Seems Gus has a guest," said Hilma.

Fanny felt a cold draft. She opened her eyes and looked around. "Brrrr, I hate this house," she said then tucked herself up into a tight ball and closed her eyes again.

Kit Kat pounced on Fanny. Fanny's head shot up; the cold draft was stronger. She got up and moved to the foot of the bed.

Hilma laughed. Kit Kat growled. Hilma reached down and petted Fanny. Fanny squirmed from the cold touch. Kit Kat growled again.

"Oh, Kit Kat, you're jealous. How sweet! You needn't worry, my precious. This cat has many lives left. Besides, dear one, no other cat could ever take your place!"

Hilma floated out the door. Kit Kat followed. Together they swirled around the rooms then drifted upstairs. Hilma spied Gus on the chaise lounge and joined him there. She stretched out, her body going straight through him. Gus shivered and jumped down.

"Why do you do that to me, Hilma?" said Gus shaking his head. He plopped down on a rug. Kit Kat curled up next to him. "Geez, Kit Kat, not so close. You're making me cold." Kit Kat nosed Gus's back, Gus squirmed.

"Ah, Kit Kat, I remember lazy afternoons lying on this lovely chaise lounge," said Hilma. "I would have a nice cold glass of ice tea, in the summer of course, or a hot mug of cocoa in winter."

"Oh, brother," whispered Gus.

Kit Kat hopped up on the lounge and snuggled against Hilma. She ruffled the cat's fur. Kit Kat purred.

 "You were so amusing back then," said Hilma. "I remember sitting right here watching out the window as you chased after a bird. It was some loud squawking blue jay if memory serves. Up the tree

19

you went." Hilma paused and rested her hand on Kit Kat's head. "You would have caught it too if that old branch hadn't given way." Kit Kat stopped purring. "Oh, sorry love. I forgot. You lost one of your lives that day." She hooked her finger under the cat's jaw and lifted her head. "But you learned to land on your feet the next time, didn't you?" Kit Kat purred again.

Hilma absent-mindedly petted Kit Kat, all the while gazing out the window. The house was quiet and Gus was lightly snoring. Suddenly Hilma let out a shrill giggle that levitated Gus right off the floor. "Oh, goody! Oh, goody! Oh, goody!" Hilma exclaimed. She flew in rapid circles around the room leaving Kit Kat spinning like a top on the chaise lounge. "Look, Kit Kat, my little darling. Trespassers! We don't like trespassers, do we?" She scooped Kit Kat up and twirled her around. "But they can be such good sport! Come, my pet! Let's have a little fun!" Hilma evaporated through the floorboards.

Kit Kat poked her head through the glass and spied three skinny young boys walking up the driveway. She flew through the floor to join Hilma.

Gus looked out the window and spotted the boys. "Trespassers all right. I almost feel sorry for them."

The boys circled around to the back of the house.

The tallest boy waved a flashlight casting light on the trees, bushes and the house. The smallest boy collected pine cones in a makeshift pouch he had made with the front of his shirt. The tall boy shined the light on the attic window and said to the small boy, "Okay, Kenny, you have to break the glass with one of those pine cones. I hope you picked up some hard green ones."

"I've changed my mind. I don't want to, Steven," said Kenny to the tall boy with the flashlight.

Steven waved the light in Kenny's face. "Do you want to join our club, or don't you?" He turned to the third boy. "I knew he would chicken out. Alex, your little brother is a wimp."

Alex patted Kenny on the back. "Wind up and give it a toss. You can do it."

"What if we get caught, Alex?" said Kenny.

Steven shined the flashlight under his chin making a spooky face. "Hurry up and do it, Kenny!"

Kenny looked to his brother. Alex gave him the thumbs up. Kenny pulled a pine cone from his collection. His whole body was shaking. "Are you sure, Alex?" said Kenny. Alex nodded his head. He turned to Steven. Steven threw his arms up in the air causing the light from the flashlight to shine off a fir tree. "It's now or never, wimp," said Steven. Kenny tossed a pine cone. It bounced off the house missing the window. He threw a second and a third, none hitting the window. "The cones aren't heavy enough to get that high," Kenny whined.

Steven picked up a rock from the driveway. "Last chance, Kenny. Pitch this and break that window or you can never be in the club!" He handed the rock to Kenny.

Kenny shifted the rock back and forth from one hand to the other. Staring at Steven, he leaned back and wound up to throw. Just at that moment Hilma's deep mournful cry blasted from inside the house. Kenny flung the rock. It whizzed past Steven's head. Steven screamed and ran down the driveway, his flashlight abandoned on the ground shining in the grass where he had dropped it.

Alex tripped over his own feet trying to run away. He low-crawled across the lawn, and stopped at the road. "Come on, Kenny!"

Kenny stood frozen in place staring in a window. Four glowing yellow eyes stared back at him. Then Kit Kat flew at the window, her fur puffed out all over her body, her tail stretched straight up. Hilma cackled and drifted into the living room where she lighted on the piano stool. She threw her head back and screeched, moaned, and howled in a most musical voice, her ghostly fingers dissolving through the piano keys, unable to play a single note. Kit Kat darted about the room.

Alex yelled, "Kenny! Come on Kenny!" He ran back, took Kenny's hand, and dragged him away.

Hilma floated off the piano stool. "All is well! They've run off. Come, sweet companion. Let's see what

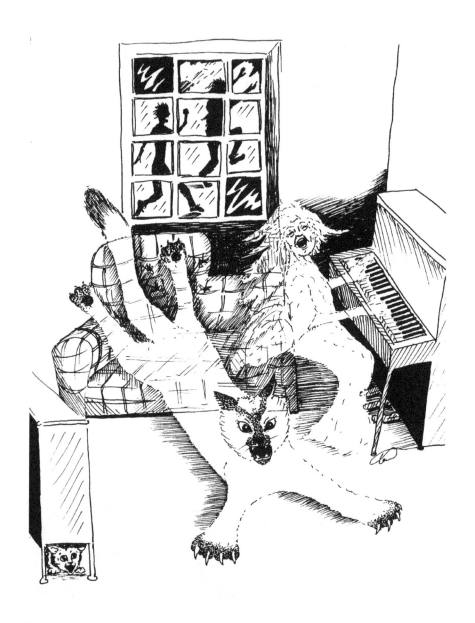

Monsieur Bouquet is up to." Hilma drifted through the floorboards to the basement. Kit Kat looked out at the empty driveway, then flew to the bedroom to pester Fanny again.

Hilma's chilling voice thundered from the basement. "Kit Kat! Come!" Kit Kat stopped flying, blinked, then dissolved through the floorboards.

Upstairs, Gus groaned. He shouted to Fanny, "SEE YOU IN THE MORNING!"

"See you in the morning, that's funny. Only if you have x-ray vision, Gus." Fanny stretched out on the afghan, licked her paw, and cleaned her whiskers. "Anyway, Tess will come back soon. I can't get out of here fast enough."

"WHAT?" said Gus.

"GOOD NIGHT!" said Fanny.

"GOOD NIGHT!" said Gus. *Good night, Hilma. Good night, Kit Kat. Please, let the rest of tonight be quiet.*

Buzz Buzz

Fanny woke. Her eyes squinted against the sunlight glaring in through a dirty window. She looked around the room. Along one wall sat a vanity with a tall, oval mirror. A tarnished silver hand mirror and glittering jewels spilling over from an open jewelry box were arranged on top. Across the room stood a white bureau. One of the eight drawers was pulled out. A red silk scarf dangled from it. A closet door was ajar. Fanny could see more than a dozen pairs of women's shoes neatly lined up on the floor inside. *I like this room,* Fanny thought.

She heard buzzing and spied a bug flying outside the window. She noted that the insect's abdomen hung down behind its slender body. As the sun warmed the house, the buzzing grew louder. A multitude of the insects began to fly back and forth outside the window. *Wasps! Are you kidding? Please, please come and get me out of here, Tess!*

She padded out of the room, snatched a few bites of kibble, and gulped down a long drink of water before going to the door at the bottom of the stairs. "GUS?"

Gus was watching a pair of squirrels run up and down an oak tree gathering acorns. Without looking away he yelled back, "YEAH, FANNY!" The squirrels froze, their tiny faces zeroed in on Gus.

"Danger! Cat!" the squirrels chattered in unison.

Gus stood up on the bed, arched his back, and stretched. The squirrels continued to chatter their alarm. Gus hopped down to the floor and walked out of the room. The squirrels looked at each other, shrugged their little shoulders, and went back to work.

Gus trotted to the bottom of the stairs. "Good morning, Fanny."

"What's good about it, Gus?"

"Is your bowl half empty or half full, Fanny?"

Fanny cocked her head to the side. "What are you talking about, half empty or half full? My bowl is as full as I've ever seen it before, a fact that worries me a little."

Gus stretched up and clawed the door casing. "It means, are you happy about what you have, or unhappy about what you don't have?"

Fanny groomed herself. She looked around the room and out the window. "Right now? I am very unhappy about what I don't have. I don't have my box on the patio with the green rug, or my box on the front porch with the pink blanket, or my cushion high up on the sailboat where I can see forever, or my smooth warm rock next to the pond that is filled with bright orange fish. What I do have is this house of horrors."

Gus stopped clawing the wood. "Oh, I see."

Fanny put her head down on her paws. "I don't belong in a dilapidated old place like this."

"You might have your deck box, porch box, sailboat and pond, but I have this wonderful historical monument. It's filled with soft beds, couches, chairs, and my chaise lounge. I have a big barn with warm, dry hay and a tractor with a soft seat. I have fields and woods and even a creek!"

"Yeah, yeah, yeah. Blah, blah, blah. The sooner I get out of this place, the happier I'll be," said Fanny.

"You go ahead and have a bad attitude. The sooner you're gone and Peggy comes back, the happier I'll be."

Fanny wasn't listening any longer.

Squeak Squeak

Fanny's ears picked up scurrying sounds coming from the kitchen. She crept toward the noise. She froze in place when she caught sight of a small mouse dancing across the counter. She stared intently at it as it hopped on the water faucet then tiptoed out over the sink and put its head at the spout to swallow the drip. Fanny took careful slow steps toward the mouse, then with lightning speed she jumped on the counter.

The mouse flew to the floor and scampered under an electric range. Fanny was undaunted. She jumped down, crouched on the floor in front of the range, and waited.

Gus paced back and forth on his side of the door. "What's going on?"

"Mouse!" Fanny called. "He's hiding." She peered under the range and saw two beady little eyes staring back at her. "But you can't hide forever," she hissed at the mouse.

The mouse believed her. Marvin squeaked, "Where did this cat come from, Gus?"

"Fanny, that's Marvin Mouse. He lives here too. He's my friend," said Gus.

30

"Gus, you have some unusual friends," said Fanny.

Gus attempted to explain the situation to Fanny. "Marvin has gotten me out of more than one tangled mess. We have a truce. I don't bother him; he and his family don't bother my food. It works for us."

Fanny was zeroed in on Marvin, her gaze unwavering. Marvin's whole body trembled.

Gus paced back and forth on his side of the door. "Fanny, I'd really like you to leave the little guy alone."

Fanny ignored him. She hovered, still as a statue, the tips of the fur on her belly touching the floor. Her tail laid straight out behind her, twitching slightly at its tip. She felt something pinch it, then heard a squeak. She whirled around just in time to see another mouse skitter away across the floor and under an old gas heater. She chased after it giving Marvin the opportunity to dart out from under the kitchen range and into a hole in the wall. He scurried between the walls and out another hole to join Gus on the staircase.

Marvin was wheezing. "Gus, where did that cat come from?" He stuck his tiny face under the door and watched Fanny. "Marcia! Are you ok?" Marvin called.

Gus shook his head. "Fanny!"

"Not now, Gus," Fanny hissed.

Marcia peeked out from under the heater. In a high pitched voice she squeaked, "Where did this cat come from?"

Marvin darted out into the room. Fanny spun around. Marcia made it to the hole in the wall and Marvin slid under the old piano.

Fanny sat on her haunches and groomed herself. Marvin made a hasty retreat to the stairwell. Marcia and Marvin huddled together, noses twitching.

"Tell me again about the truce you have with these mice," said Fanny.

Gus sighed. "Marvin saved me from certain death. Peggy was miffed at the birds eating the raspberries in her garden and draped a net over the plants. One evening I chased after a blue jay and got tangled in the netting. The more I tried to get free, the tighter the net wrapped around me."

"So the little guy chewed through and set you free?" Fanny asked.

"As a matter of fact, he did! And just in the nick of time! Howling, snarling, hungry coyotes were coming for me." Gus high-fived Marvin. "Now, I let Marvin and Marcia live here in my house." He winked at the mice, "Provided they don't eat or otherwise mess with my food."

"That is a very touching story Gus, but if you dispatch them to mouse heaven, you don't need any truce."

The mice quivered up against the wall away from the door.

"Sheesh, Fanny!" said Gus. "When someone saves your life, you owe them a life. And, anyway, Marvin and Marcia are my friends."

"Ok, ok, I get it. Why don't you send those two out here so I can get a good look and smell of them? If they are so important to you, I don't want to accidentally confuse them with some other random mice and do them any harm."

The mice shook their heads "no" emphatically. "Go ahead," Gus coaxed.

Marvin nudged Marcia. Gus silently mouthed, "Go on." The two mice crawled out. Fanny stared at them.

"Fanny, this is Marvin and Marcia," said Gus from behind the door.

The mice bowed. Fanny opened her mouth in a wide yawn showing her sharp teeth. The mice skittered back under the door, past Gus, and ducked through the hole in the wall. Gus could hear the tiny scratching sounds of the two scurrying away.

"I would appreciate it if you wouldn't mess with the status quo, Fanny," said Gus.

"Don't worry, Gus. I wouldn't DREAM of hurting your little friends."

Mew Mew

The sound of crunching gravel outside the house had Gus up the stairs in a flash.

"Oh, brother, here we go again," said Fanny. "Does it ever stop?" She hopped up on the back of a couch and poked her head out between the dusty lace curtains.

Upstairs, Gus jumped on a pile of boxes to see out the window. "IT'S OK, FANNY!" he shouted. A meter reader from the gas company parked a truck in the driveway and walked to the side of the house, clipboard in hand. "THAT MAN COMES HERE OFTEN. HE IS A FRIEND."

Fanny rolled her eyes. "Drama, drama, drama." The man looked up and saw Fanny. She jerked her head back, hopped down from the couch, padded over to Gus's door, and settled herself on the floor. "How did you happen to end up living here?" She looked around the room. "In this place you seem to love so much." She yawned and listened to Gus's footfalls coming down the stairs. "Where is the rest of your family?"

Gus stretched up tall and leaned against the door casing. He scratched the wood. Satisfied he'd put a fine point on his sharp claws, he plopped down on his side of the door. "I wasn't born here. Fate brought me here."

"So, living here is your destiny?" Fanny laughed.

"Laugh if you want." Gus sat up straight. "Before I came here I lived with my mother, sisters, and brothers." Gus paused. "We had a little mistress, Mandy, who kept us in a box in her garage. She was gentle. I liked her very much."

"So, why did you come here?" Fanny asked.

Gus put his head on his paws. "It wasn't exactly my idea. One night when I was a little kitten, smooshed between my brothers and sisters sleeping in our big cardboard box, we were kidnapped."

"Seriously?" said Fanny.

Gus scratched his ear. "Well, maybe not kidnapped. We were abducted."

"That's the same thing, Gus."

Gus cleared his throat. "The night we were taken I heard Mandy's father walk in the garage from the house. He smelled like cooked chicken and cigarette smoke."

"Eeeww!" Fanny exclaimed.

"'Here, kitty, kitty, kitty,' he said, then coughed like he had a bone stuck in his throat. My mother growled then she hopped out of the box and ran away. One of my sisters mewed. I looked up out of the box just as a lid came down and covered the opening. Mandy's father groaned, and I felt our box tilt and wobble. We kept bumping into each other and falling down when we tried to stand up in the moving box."

"So, you were taken from the garage by your mistress's father and brought here?"

"No, not here. When all the bouncing and bumping inside the box finally stopped that night, and the top of the box was pulled off, I saw Mandy's father's face. I felt his hand wrap around my belly. He pulled me out and put me on the ground with my litter mates. His car rolled away and there I was, huddling

close to my sisters and brothers on the side of a road crying. Barks, howls, shrieks and the crunch of tires rolling by, terrified me. One by one, my siblings ran off. I chased after my brother, but I lost him in thorny bushes. The deeper I inched into the brambles, the more lost I got, until I couldn't see any way out."

Fanny shuddered.

"I finally stopped in a tiny space, where large blackberry stalks with angry thorns surrounded me. I stayed crouched into a tight ball all that night. When daylight came I started crying. I couldn't help it. I guess I worked up to a loud wail, because Rob, that's Peggy's man, heard me. When I heard him chopping through the briars, getting closer and closer, and his big hand came down and circled around my belly, I was so relieved, I didn't even think about being scared. I went limp. He carried me out and handed me to Peggy. I've been here on this farm ever since."

Fanny stretched out on her side, her nose at the crack at the bottom of the door. "So, it was your destiny to become a farm cat."

Gus shook his head. "I guess you could call me a farm cat. I prefer Master Guard Cat."

"Of course you do," said Fanny.

The cats sat in silence, each on their side of the closed door, listening to the sounds of the old house and the wind outside. After a few peaceful minutes Gus asked, "So, Fanny, where's the rest of your family? Have you always lived with Tess?"

Fanny got up, stretched, sat on her haunches, licked her paw, and cleaned her face. "The only family I ever had was my mother and she left me under a porch somewhere and never came back."

"Your mother left you? That is horrible," said Gus.

"I was born during the cold season, Gus. The time of year when cold rain starts in the morning and doesn't stop all day. Or, when the sky is blue, but the ground is frozen and hard. Or, when snow covers everything. I was a little kitten when my mother left me."

"What kind of a mother would do that?"

"We didn't live in a garage with a Mandy to care for us! My mother was a good mother and I loved her very much!"

"Sorry, Fanny," said Gus.

"My mother made a nice place for us under a porch. She used to always say to me, 'Stay here and be quiet. I'm going to get us some good food. I'll be back soon.'

One morning she left like she always did, but by nightfall she hadn't come back. She didn't come back that night or the next day, so I ventured out into the cold wet world to find her."

"I'm not sure that was the best thing to do," said Gus.

"What else was I supposed to do? She probably needed my help."

"I suppose I would have done the same thing."

"As I was saying, I left to go find her. Right off the bat a big black dog chased me through a snowy yard, so I clawed my way to the top of a fence post, all the while the dog nipping at my tail. He sat at the bottom of the post barking and barking until a car drove past, and he chased after it trying to bite its tires. Stupid dog! I kept looking for my mother, wandering across yards, sniffing around houses. I climbed up into a fir tree and hunkered down trying to warm myself, but that didn't last very long. A big raccoon charged up the tree hissing at me. I dove off the branch, landed on my four feet, and ran. I followed along the side of a road while passing cars splattered me with slush. I figured I was a goner and I would never find my mother. I gave up and laid down in the wet slush."

"You're making me shiver just thinking about that."

"Oh, I bet you've never been that cold, Gus!"

Gus ignored that remark. "What happened next?"

"Well, I was crying in the snow beside the road when Tess stopped her car, got out, and picked me up. She tucked me inside her coat. It was warm there and I could hear her heart beating. I was weak and hungry. I tried not to, but I fell asleep."

"That's nice," said Gus. He stretched out on his side of the door.

"Tess brought me to her house. She cradled me in her arm while piling scraps of carpet on the floor of her garage. She put me down on top of that pile then brought a bowl filled with milk and set it alongside me. She had other cats. I could hear them. They patrolled the area, sniffing around the doors. I saw them watching me through the windows. If they came into the garage, I hid. I only ventured out of hiding when I knew nobody was watching me. The other cats got used to my presence and left me alone. Tess propped the door open so I could leave, but the outside world frightened me. Even Tess frightened me. I thought she might leave me out in the cold the same way my mother did. I stayed hidden in the garage until Tess's man Jack started coming to sit with me. Jack was so calm. He was the first person to recognize how pretty I was, and he sang songs about my beauty."

Gus covered his face with his paw. *This cat is something else,* he thought.

"Jack convinced me it would be just fine to come out. I had a home there and was welcome."

"Things just have a way of working out, don't they?" said Gus.

"Yeah, well, now Tess has stuck me in this ramshackle old place! She'd better have a really good explanation for why I've been sequestered here! Jack will be angry when he finds out his Princess Fantas-ti-cat is missing, that's all I've got to say. "

"Sequestered! Ramshackle! I'm here! You be careful, missy, or I just might stop talking to you. Then you'll really be alone. And, I keep telling you, this house is a Historical Monument. They don't make farmhouses like this any longer." Gus trotted up the stairs muttering, "Princess Fantas-ti-cat, sheesh."

Hilma sat on the couch with Kit Kat in her lap. "Such sad stories. What do you think, Kit Kat? Should we feel sorry for her?"

Kit Kat shook her head "no". She floated over to Fanny, then flew quick circles around and through her. Fanny got up and ran to the couch. She didn't know it, but she'd settled herself alongside Hilma. Hilma reached down and petted her. Kit Kat squeezed herself between Hilma and Fanny. Hilma laughed. Fanny shivered, jumped down, and ran under the cabinet.

 "Gus!" Fanny called.

Gus ignored her.

Puff Puff

"What do you suppose our little pole cat is up to, Kit Kat?" Hilma asked. "Let's take a turn about the house, then drop in on Monsieur 'Bud' Bouquet."

They found Bud lying in the soft cool dirt under the back porch. Kit Kat squatted in front of him and pressed her nose against the sleeping skunk's nose. Hilma swooped over Bud, sniffed the skunk's tail, and said, "Phew, Bud, you've puffed."

Bud lifted his head and blinked his eyes. "I didn't know ghosts could smell."

"You're correct, Budkins," said Hilma. "I really can't smell that pungent odor of yours anymore." She threw her head back and cackled. Bud cowered. She stopped laughing and smoothed her hair away from her face. "I saw the great horned owl, Spike, from the window last night. I thought you may have had to let loose some of your acrid spray on him." She motioned to Kit Kat, "For heaven's sake, come here my naughty kitty. Don't be bothering our little friend. Can't you see Bud had a bad night?" Kit Kat flew to Hilma's arms.

"Oh, Hilma, it WAS a bad night. My stomach was rumbling something awful. I didn't have any luck finding the tiniest bit of supper. I wanted to join Fingers and his gang on the deck next door for some kitty kibble. Just a nibble or two was all I was asking for, but they hissed, called me names, and chased me away."

"Oh, Buddy, I'm sorry," said Hilma. "I guess they haven't forgiven you for spraying on the kibble last time you joined them."

"That was an accident, Hilma. They scared me." Bud hung his head and drew circles in the dirt with his claw. "I've apologized a hundred times."

Hilma wagged her pointer finger in Bud's face. "Your apologies did not make the food edible, Buddly. To make matters worse, the neighbors didn't put food out on the deck for weeks after that."

"I know, I know," said Bud. He covered his face with his paw.

"So, Monsieur, tell me, did the owl bother you last night?"

Bud peeked out from under his paw. "Yup, Spike did." Bud stood up on his hind legs, stretched his front legs out and ran in circles. "Spike flew over top of me like this." He kept running then hopped up and down on his back feet. "Spike reached his talons for my back like this. I felt them comb through the fur on my back. He scared me." Bud sat down.

"Not enough time to spray?" said Hilma.

"Sometimes my tail has a mind of its own. I sprayed. I sprayed a big puff . . . I missed."

"Oh! Sorry Monsieur."

"I ran to a tree and Spike had to fly around it. I saw him circling back to get me. I may have puffed again, I'm not sure. I ran under the tractor that Rob left out in the garden. I waited until I couldn't see him anymore and high-tailed it home. I think Spike is real mad at me now."

"I'm sure you did high-tail it home, Monsieur Bouquet. I'm sure you did," said Hilma. "Better luck tonight, my stinky little friend."

"Oh no. I won't be going out tonight. It feels like a storm is coming."

"A storm, eh?" Hilma mused.

Boom Boom

Hilma drifted into the first floor bedroom. She stopped at the vanity and gazed into the oval mirror, but saw no reflection. She sighed. She moved to the bureau and touched the silk scarf peeking from the drawer, then settled herself in the window seat. Fanny sneezed. Hilma looked at the cat snuggled down in a frayed afghan on the bed. Fanny mumbled something, but appeared to go back to sleep. Hilma turned her gaze to the window. No wind blew through the trees, no bats darted about above the garden, no bugs buzzed, no frogs croaked, no crickets chirped. It was dead still, eerily quiet. Clouds hid the moon and stars. The air was hot and muggy. Hilma waited. A smile played across her face when lightning flashed, bombarding the room with bright white light. She looked at Fanny. The calico cat didn't budge. Hilma counted, *one one-thousand, two one-thousand, three one-thousand, four one-thousand.* BOOM! Thunder rumbled shaking the house.

Fanny popped her head up and yowled, "WHAT WAS THAT?" Another flash of lightning, and Fanny hunkered down on the bed, "GUS!"

Hilma counted, *one one-thousand, two one-thousand, three one-thousand.* BOOM! Thunder rumbled louder than before. *Getting closer.* She watched Fanny squirm deeper under the afghan. "Poor, frightened little kitty." She poked her hand through the crocheted yarn and touched Fanny.

"GUS!" Fanny yowled.

Kit Kat drifted into the room and lit on Hilma's lap. She watched Fanny, then snickered.

"I know what you're thinking, Kit Kat," said Hilma. "You're thinking Fanny is a scaredy-cat tangling herself up in my old afghan like that." Kit Kat nodded her head up and down.

A blaze of white light filled the room, followed quickly by a boom that rattled the house, dropping pictures from the walls, knocking chairs over, emptying cupboards of their dishes, and bookcases of their books. Fanny cried out, "Gus, help me!"

"It's getting closer, my pet." said Hilma. "Come along. It's time to check on Gus."

Gus was pacing back and forth on the chaise lounge. Lightning flashed and thunder cracked at the same time. The house shook violently, throwing Gus to the floor. Seconds later a huge fir tree was struck by lightning, cracking and breaking it. It smashed down on the house, collapsing the roof and walls. Broken boards and tree branches trapped Gus. Hilma hurried to Gus and tried to pry the broken boards away to free him. Her ghostly hands and arms were useless.

Smoke was filling the house. In the bedroom downstairs Fanny was fighting to free herself from the afghan. The more she struggled the tighter it became. "GUS!" she yowled over and over.

From upstairs Gus could hear her. He yowled back, "I'm coming! I'm coming!" and pushed and scratched at the splintered wood that imprisoned him.

Fingers had been waddling across the attic when the tree hit. He felt the wind of the giant tree slamming down through the roof and had to jump to avoid falling through the floor with it. He peered over the edge at the destruction, shook his fur, lifted his paw, and twisted the pinky ring around on his finger. "Sheesh!" He picked his way across what was left of the attic and hopped down into the room with Gus. It was dark and smoky. He yelled, "Gus! Tony sent me over here to save your skinny cat hide."

"Fingers! Fingers? Is that you? I'm here! I'm stuck!"

Fingers followed Gus's voice to a pile of boards covering the chaise lounge. "You're trapped pretty good there, Gus." He laughed. "What's it worth to you, if I get you free?"

"Fingers! I've never been so happy to hear your voice. Get me out of here! You can have all my kibble for a week."

The smoke was getting thicker. "To my way a thinkin'
a week's worth ain't enough. Maybe a month's worth
and I'll consider it. The place is on fire here, Gus."
Fingers pulled and pried at the boards trapping Gus,
but he couldn't move them. He grunted, "I'm putting
my life on the line for you here, buddy."

"Whatever you want, Fingers," said Gus.

Fanny called from downstairs. "Gus! Gus!"

Gus pushed harder on the boards. "Never mind me, Fingers. Go save Fanny."

"I'm not leaving you and going after that calico pussy cat, Gus. Tony'd have MY hide. Don't worry, I'll get you out of here, then you can go save her your own self." Fingers tried a different spot. The board moved. He yanked it up, threw it aside, and pulled on the next.

"Hurry, Fingers!"

Meanwhile, the little bedroom downstairs was quickly filling with dark black smoke. The only clear air was on the floor. Fanny was wound tight in the afghan. She couldn't get out. "Gus, Gus," she cried weaker with each breath.

Marvin and Marcia popped through a hole in the bedroom wall. They were scurrying through the room when they heard Fanny. They looked at each other, then crawled up on the bed. Marvin shook his head and started to scamper off. Marcia grabbed his tail and yanked him back. "We could help her," Marcia said and nodded toward Fanny. "Gus would want us to." They both stared at Fanny winding herself up tighter and tighter. "For Gus," they said in unison and started chewing through the strands of yarn. Fanny watched in disbelief. The mice made a hole big enough to free Fanny, but she wouldn't move. Marvin squeaked at Fanny, "Run for your life." Fanny still would not move. Marcia bit Fanny's tail. Fanny blinked. Marvin hopped up and down on the bed, pointed to the floor and said, "Follow us!"

Upstairs, Fingers cleared an opening for Gus. He grabbed Gus by the scruff of his neck and pulled him out. Gus gaped at the bright orange flames licking the fallen tree and the house. "We have to free Fanny!"

"We have to get out of here, buddy. I already told ya I get paid to protect you, not your little girlfriend," Fingers said. "Time is running out, my friend."

"I have to save her," Gus said.

"Suit yourself. I'm outta here." Fingers waddled away.

Gus didn't have time to argue. He clawed his way down the burning tree, flames singeing his fur. He called her name over and over, "Fanny! Fanny!"

Hilma sat on the living room couch with Kit Kat watching the destruction of her house. She saw Gus inching across the room and flew to him. "Let me help you. Follow in my chilly path."

"I'm trying to find Fanny, Hilma. Where is she?"

"Follow me," said Hilma.

Fanny had jumped down from the bed, but she'd lost sight of the mice in the dark smoke. She bumped into the wall, then inched along it moving away from the heat. The wall ended at the door to the kitchen. "Gus!" she called.

Gus heard her and called from the living room, "Fanny!"

Fanny entered the kitchen moving toward Gus's voice when she slammed into Bud. "Eeeewwwwww!" Fanny yowled.

Crumbs flew from his mouth as Monsieur Bouquet mumbled, "You made me stink!" He hung his little skunk head. "It's your fault. I didn't want to puff. You scared me. All I wanted was a couple bites of your kibble. You made me stink."

Hilma guided Gus into the kitchen. The smoke and skunk spray made it hard for Gus to breathe. He squinted his eyes and took shallow breaths. "Bud?"

"I'm here," Bud said.

Gasping, Gus said, "I'm looking for a cat."

"Oh, she went that way." Bud pointed to the door. "I'm awful sorry, Gus. She made me puff."

Flames were boiling into the kitchen from the living room. "Get out of the house, Bud. You can apologize later," said Gus.

Fanny stopped looking for Gus when she saw an open door. She charged through it and found herself outside. She gulped a few big breaths of fresh air, then ran.

Gus and Bud tumbled out the door. Gus spotted Fanny and chased after her all the while calling her name. She didn't stop running, but turned and looked back at him. Little did she know, she was running straight for a 40 foot deep hole.

"Kit Kat!" yelled Hilma. "The well! Fanny is headed straight for the well!" Kit Kat flew to Fanny, but what could a Siamese ghost cat do? One paw dangling in mid-air, Fanny was about to fall to her certain death.

Kit Kat couldn't grab her and pull her to safety. Kit Kat did the only thing she could do, she flew through Fanny. Her cold touch made Fanny veer away, narrowly missing the well, and sent the terrified cat racing down the driveway.

Hilma sighed. "Thank goodness, Kit Kat, my precious. You've saved the day. Gus would not have been pleased if that silly, calico cat had fallen into the well and drowned." Kit Kat jumped into Hilma's arms and together they floated back into the burning house. "I don't know what Gus sees in her, do you?" said Hilma. Kit Kat shrugged. They flew from room to room, then came back and watched from the back porch as all their animal friends scurried away. Hilma sighed again. "Kit Kat, they're all gone. We're all alone again. Soon the house will be gone too." She hung her head. Just then, far off in the distance, sirens were screaming. The sound grew louder and louder. Hilma raised her head, her eyes glowed yellow. Big red fire trucks with bright, blinking, red and white lights on top, roared up the driveway. Handsome men in yellow turnouts and helmets spilled out. They scurried around the house dragging hoses and spraying water. "Oh, Kit Kat, isn't this exciting!"

It started to rain big, fat, bounce-off-the-ground drops. The time between lightning flashes and thunder booms was growing longer. Gus dodged around the fire trucks rolling up the driveway. He caught sight of Fanny as she swerved and narrowly missed being flattened by the right front tire of a moving truck. He lost her for a few seconds. Then he saw her ducking into a ditch beside the road. Gus dug in and ran at cheetah speed after her. Fanny heard something chasing her. It spooked her. She screeched to a halt and turned to attack. Gus put on his brakes. He skidded right into her. Gus was out of breath. "This way, Fanny," he wheezed. The skunk spray on Fanny's fur made his eyes water and his nose burn. "This way!" Gus stepped away from her and motioned. "We need to get to the barn. This way!"

"Why should I follow you?" said Fanny. She waited until he'd taken a few steps, licked her paw, spat out the foul skunk spray from her tongue, shook her head, and then followed. They circled out around the house, then cut across the garden.

WHAM! Fanny was broadsided by a flying tomato and fell to the ground. WHAM! A second tomato hit, splattering her side. Gus looked in every direction. WHAM! A third tomato struck. Gus saw the culprit. "Fingers! What are you doing? Stop that!"

Fingers was standing in the garden, a fourth tomato in his paw. He pulled back and threw but this time Gus stepped in front of the incoming tomato bomb to shield Fanny. Fingers yelled, "Get out of the way, Gus."

"Stop throwing tomatoes at us," said Gus.

"I'm not throwing them at you, I'm throwing them at your stinky girlfriend," said Fingers. "Now move."

"Why are you doing this? Stop!"

Fingers wound up and threw a big soft one. It hit the ground and splashed both cats. "Don't you know tomatoes gets rid of the putridness of Bud's puffs? I'm doing us all a favor."

Gus sniffed Fanny. Fanny sniffed herself. Between the rain and the tomato's juice, both cats were soaked. They started to laugh. Fingers twisted his gold ring around his pinky, then waddled off shaking his head. Gus stopped laughing and looked at the charred house. Pale, gray smoke and steam boiled in the air. Firefighters were still soaking the walls and roof with streams of water from the thick white hoses.

Fanny looked at Gus's sad face. *The Master Guard Cat looks pretty handsome even soaking wet,* she thought. She shook, sending a red spray out from her body. "Wet fur is the worst," she said. Gus shook out his own fur. "The worst," he said.

"I'm sorry about your farmhouse. I know how proud you were of the place," said Fanny.

Gus bumped Fanny shoulder to shoulder and said, "Come on, Fanny. It's going to be all right. Peggy and Rob will take care of the house. Let me show you the barn. You're going to love it. It's a historical monument!"

The End

Made in the USA
Columbia, SC
26 January 2024

30115911R10036